Peter Easter Frog

Erin Dealey   Illustrated by G. Brian Karas

A Caitlyn Dlouhy Book
Atheneum Books for Young Readers
NEW YORK   LONDON   TORONTO   SYDNEY   NEW DELHI

atheneum

ATHENEUM BOOKS FOR YOUNG READERS

An imprint of Simon & Schuster Children's Publishing Division

1230 Avenue of the Americas, New York, New York 10020

Text © 2021 by Erin Dealey

Illustrations © 2021 by G. Brian Karas

Book design by Greg Stadnyk © 2021 by Simon & Schuster, Inc.

ATHENEUM BOOKS FOR YOUNG READERS is a registered trademark of Simon & Schuster, Inc. Atheneum logo is a trademark of Simon & Schuster, Inc.

For information about special discounts for bulk purchases, please contact Simon & Schuster Special Sales at 1-866-506-1949 or business@simonandschuster.com.

The Simon & Schuster Speakers Bureau can bring authors to your live event. For more information or to book an event, contact the Simon & Schuster Speakers

Bureau at 1-866-248-3049 or visit our website at www.simonspeakers.com.

The text for this book was set in Gill Sans and Okay Crayon.

The illustrations for this book were rendered in mixed media.

Manufactured in China

1020 SCP

First Edition

10 9 8 7 6 5 4 3 2 1

Library of Congress Cataloging-in-Publication Data

Names: Dealey, Erin, author. | Karas, G. Brian, illustrator.

Title: Peter Easter Frog / Erin Dealey ; illustrated by G. Brian Karas.

Description: First edition. | New York : Atheneum, [2021] | "A Caitlyn Dlouhy Book." | Summary: A frog named Peter, who loves Easter, decides to deliver some eggs,

with the help of his friends, but when The Bunny finds out, he is not pleased.

Identifiers: LCCN 2018046692 | ISBN 9781481464895 (hardcover : alk. paper) | ISBN 9781481464925 (eBook)

Subjects: | CYAC: Easter—Fiction. | Frogs—Fiction. | Domestic animals—Fiction. | Easter Bunny—Fiction.

Classification: LCC PZ7.D339239 Pet 2021 | DDC [E]—dc23

LC record available at https://lccn.loc.gov/2018046692

Endless gratitude to Caitlyn Dlouhy, for believing in me from the beginning.

♡ to PRZ, G&S, and Deborah Warren
—E. D.

For Sebastian, Kassandra, Gloria, & Stephen
—G. B. K.

Here comes Peter Easter Frog,
hopping down his favorite log.

Hippity, hoppity, Easter's on its—

Hey!
You're not the bunny.

Come on! Why should Bunny have all the fun?

There goes Peter Easter Frog,

slogging through the meadow bog.

Squishity, squashity, Easter's on its—

Whoa! You're not the bunny.

I'm the Easter Frog.

Boy, can he hop!

Here comes Frog's friend Easter Cow.

Look who's helping Peter now

Clippity, cloppity, Easter's on its—

Turtle, Easter Cow, and Dog,
hiding eggs with Pete the frog.

Yippity, yappity, Easter's on its—

Say, I'm good at hiding things. . . .

Here comes Pete and all his friends.

Is this where the story ends?

Skippity, stoppity—

Uh-oh!

What do you think

Delivering eggs . . .
with Peter Easter Frog.

He LOVES Easter!
And boy, can he hop!

Haven't you ever wanted a little help?

you're doing?

Peter Who-dee Whatttt?

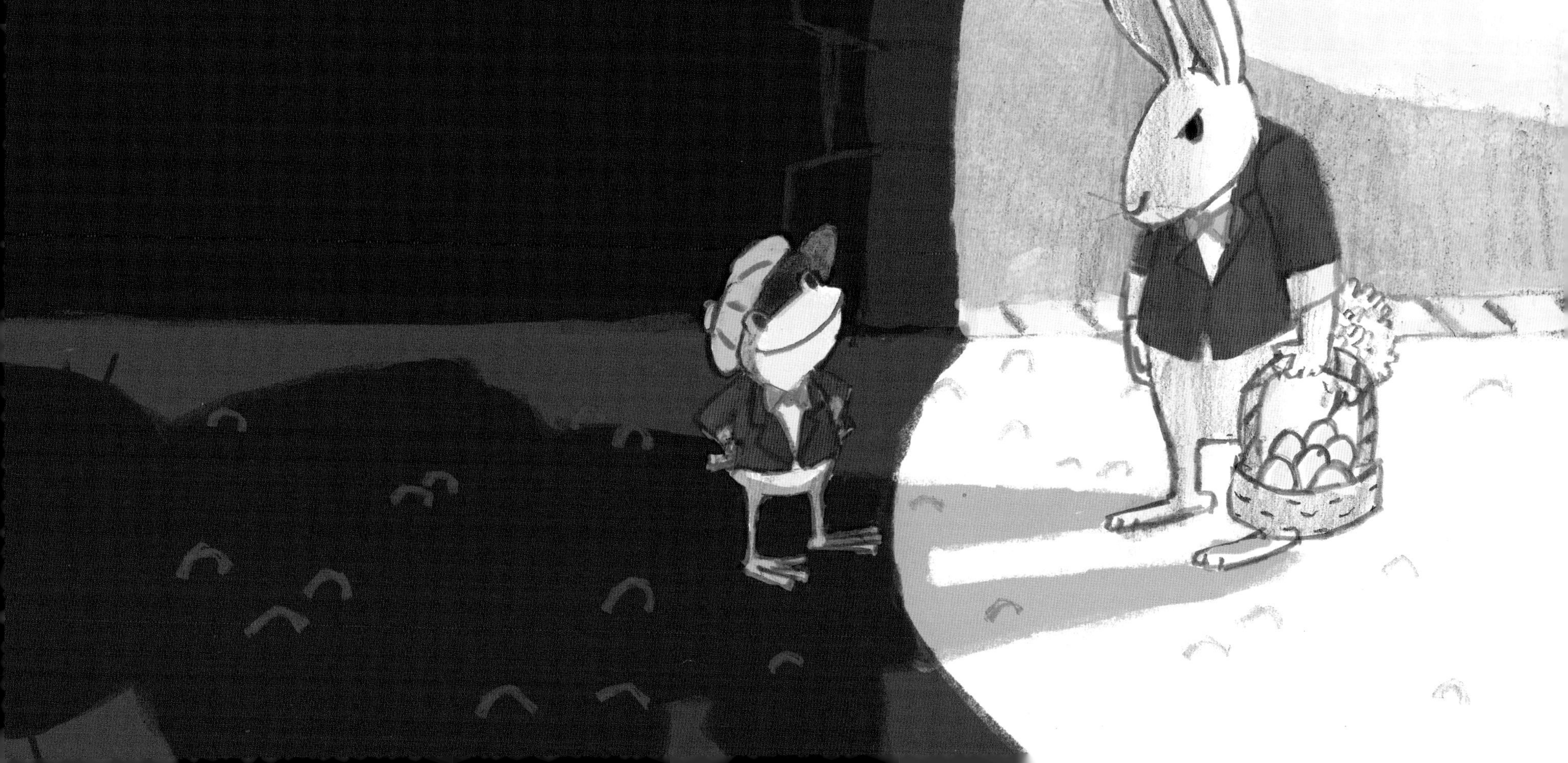

There go Peter's Easter friends.
This is where the story ends.
Sniffity—

Hold on, guys!

Cheers from Peter Easter Frog,
Chipmunk, Turtle, Cow, and Dog.
Hippity, hoppity . . .

Happy Easter Day!

ERIN DEALEY is a children's book author of many genres, from board books to young adult novels, including *Goldie Locks Has Chicken Pox* and *Little Bo Peep Can't Get to Sleep*. She grew up in Oakland, California, and lasted one full day as an employee at a pineapple factory in Hawaii. Visit her at erindealey.com.

G. BRIAN KARAS has illustrated many children's books, including *Muncha! Muncha! Muncha!* and *Tippy-Tippy-Tippy, Hide!* by Candace Fleming; *Incredible Me* by Kathi Appelt; and the High-Rise Private Eyes series by Cynthia Rylant. His books have been named ALA Notables, *Booklist* Editors' Choices, *School Library Journal* Best Books, and Boston Globe–Horn Book honor books. He lives in upstate New York. Visit him online at gbriankaras.com.